As You Wish

Lowarn Gutierrez

This is a work of fiction. Any resemblance to actual events or persons, living or dead, is entirely coincidental. Opinions expressed by characters within the book are their own and not the author's.

Please be aware that this book contains graphic depictions of self-injury and suicide.

If you are struggling with suicidal thoughts, please reach out to somebody for support.

UK
Samaritans: 116 123
CALM: 0800 58 58 58

US
National Suicide Prevention Lifeline: 1 800 273 8255
Crisis Text Line: Text HOME to 741 741

Canada
Canada Suicide Prevention Service: 1 833 456 4566
Crisis Text Line: Text HOME to 686868

Australia
Lifeline: 13 11 14
Suicide Call Back Service: 1300 659 467

For Katie

When I was 37, after nearly fifteen years of marriage, my wife died.

The day it happened is burnt into my memory forever: it felt, often, that my mind was so overtaken with it that I wasn't able to take anything in afterwards.

I had been awoken by the light streaming through a gap between the curtains onto my face, which always happened if the curtains weren't pulled into exactly the right position. After blinking myself awake, I was aware that, aside from the cat, Toasty, curled up in the crook of my knee, the bed was empty. Where was she? It was Saturday and Serena nearly always slept later than I did. As I sat up, I disturbed Toasty, who stretched a paw out towards my leg. For some reason, that movement stood out to me in my memory of the day. I often wished I'd taken it as him telling me to stay in bed.

Not that that'd have done much but delay what I was always going to find, I suppose.

Sometimes, especially when we were younger, Serena got up early to make breakfast for both of us. She liked cooking. I, for one, liked to wake up to the smell of pancakes, or bacon and eggs, or even the porridge that she'd garnish with berries and cream.

Sometimes, I'd go downstairs and find the food lukewarm and congealing on the table, and Serena would look up at me like a kicked puppy. "I called upstairs for you," she'd say, and sink into herself, wordless as I dutifully finished the plate.

That day, there'd been no scent of food or clattering in the kitchen. Toasty settled his head onto his stretched-out legs, ears twitching. Something felt off.

The bathroom was through a door adjacent to the bedroom; the door was closed. We didn't tend to lock the bathroom door unless we had guests, so the closed door was enough to signal it was occupied. She must have just needed the toilet, but I couldn't let go of my irrational anxiety. I knocked gently.

"Serena?" I called. No response. I knocked harder; called for her louder. No response.

It was then I became aware of a slip of paper on the floor, sticking out from under the door. I didn't look at it. I slammed the door open, and I found her.

She was laid back in the bath, naked, as if relaxing. She faced the ceiling, lips slightly apart, eyes nearly, but not quite, closed. One arm draped outside of the bath. The water was dark crimson. A puddle, slowly solidifying, had formed under the hand resting near the floor.

After that, I know that I called an ambulance and she was pronounced dead upon its arrival, but I don't remember any of it.

Part of me, I think, died with my wife. It drained from the bathtub along with her blood.

It had been somewhere around five years since that day, but that walk to the bathroom, seeing her, the blood on the floor, wouldn't let me go. The emptiness in the house felt endless, and I saw the whites of her lifeless eyes glinting at me through her eyelashes in the darkness of night. I kept the slip of paper in a drawer, but never had the heart to open it.

If I had been better, if I had been *more*, then maybe

she wouldn't have left like that. I hadn't had even the slightest idea she'd wanted to die. I think that's what left me so anchored to her.

Since she'd passed, I'd tried to move on, and tried to keep my connections to her positive. In the day, I worked: I'd held down my job even through the worst of my mourning by wearing a "good worker" persona like a costume, and it earnt me a decent progression through the ranks at my company. In my time off, I tried new hobbies, self-improvement, even dating.

Serena had played the viola since she was young, mostly in a local but well-renowned string quartet. She was talented, I think - I couldn't even pretend to know much at all about music. But when she played, it was beautiful. I tried to attend her performances when I didn't have work commitments. When I did, she'd greet me starry-eyed off the stage, with a joyous energy I rarely saw from her anywhere else.

The case slowly gathered dust in the corner of our bedroom. I felt as though I'd neglected her interests when she was alive. Was it so bad to try to connect with her over them now? It looked simple to play. I remembered how fluidly the bow graced the strings.

Watching her had led me to believe it was far easier than it was: the bow refused to behave in my hands. After a brief, scratchy attempt at playing, the viola was quickly and angrily returned to its case and left leaning against the wall, where she'd always kept it. It stared at me reproachfully whenever I noticed it.

Some of my personal time was spent reading self-help books. They never held the answers I wanted, but I kept buying them, hoping that, somewhere, there'd be the lesson that'd fix my life. I picked up smoking as part of an attempt to remake my image and reinvent myself, as one book advised; I used another book to help me quit. I tried a whole range of diets guaranteed to boost my mood and self-esteem, and then had to take vitamin supplements for a while after most of them.

My forays into the dating world were the least successful of all. I reckoned I was good-looking enough, and I had a good career and a cute pet cat, but no woman I met could ever compare to my wife. I knew that before even signing up for any websites. There were some women who I took out for dinner, but what could a man like me even discuss on a date? My list of failed hobbies - the viola, or my time dabbling in wellness protocols? My job - and bore them with office jargon and stories of corporate banter? My wife - and how, if only I'd been a better husband, I wouldn't be on a date at all? I couldn't bring myself to see any of them again, as lovely as some of my dates were. It didn't take long before I resigned myself to being single.

After some time, I began soliciting the services of a sex worker I found online. She had a passing resemblence to Serena - the way her light brown hair was cut into a bob with a feathery fringe; her small stature; blue-grey eyes a few shades off the real thing - and she allowed me to call her by her name. The sickness I felt deep within me in the hours afterwards meant I only visited her when I felt I'd go completely mad if I didn't, although that poor woman probably knew me better than anyone after all the time she spent listening to me sob my feelings out.

One of the only things that stuck in my desperate attempts to keep myself busy was a tendency to wander. When she was alive, Serena liked to browse shops: not just visiting high streets, but scouring the back streets of towns and cities for anything that looked exciting. Sometimes we'd end up in a cafe that felt like a slightly claustrophobic living room, or a shop that sold nothing but collectible novelty gnomes. Sometimes it'd be a second-hand bookshop that was also a bar, or a shop that sold clothes inexplicably aimed at the two specific niches of cowboys and goths. It'd been fun when she was alive, but I grew into it far more after her passing. On my own, I would imagine her pulling me along by the hand when I saw an intriguing sign or dusty shopfront, and my internal monologue would take on her voice.

I visited other women I'd have been embarrassed to be seen soliciting with on some of these adventures: namely, mediums and fortune-tellers. I had never considered myself spiritual, but the scent of incense and posters of that distinct art style depicting dragons and faeries always filled me with the hope that I could connect with Serena again.

Whether I ever did connect with her or not, I don't know. One woman, a sweet-faced lady who looked to be a little younger than me under the black eyeshadow and lipstick, drew tarot cards for me, tilting her head to one side sympathetically.

"You need to move on," she said. I didn't know if she was reading me or the cards.

"I'm trying. I can't," I choked.

Others took my obvious sadness as weakness, and would barely hide the smirk on their face and glint in their eyes when they promised clearer answers for more money, and, too often, I'd hand it over. I couldn't shake their business acumen.

With nothing, and no one, else to spend money on, I began collecting random items from the strange shops that I visited. Tacky knick-knacks and photos of people I'd never known made their homes around my house. I told myself it made the place less lonely.

A year or so after Serena's passing, people started to become impatient with me, as though I should be over it. I lost friends, and even Serena's family seemed to tire of my sadness. Surely they would know better than anyone how awful her loss felt! Soon, I had no company beyond my colleagues, who only sometimes bothered to invite me to after-work drinks, and Toasty. At least Toasty loved me unconditionally.

For a long time, I wondered where rock bottom really was, since I seemed to sink so low and yet only continued sinking; I was put onto anti-depressants that I wasn't sure helped, but which gave me strange, vivid dreams.

I took to writing down some of my dreams in a notebook kept by my bed, maybe looking for some sort of meaning, and did my best to remember and record them before wakefulness robbed me of them completely.

On a Friday night, after an unremarkable day in the office, I fell asleep quickly.

I was in a field - abandoned, or at least not in use, with the grass long and gone to seed. It was overcast, with the oppressive sensation that usually signals an oncoming storm, and it was inescapably warm. A dog was wandering some metres away from me; it hadn't noticed me yet.

Even in the dream, I was unsure what I was doing in the field. It felt like I was trespassing. The dog was big, with shaggy black fur and large, triangular ears with tips that flopped down slightly. It wasn't scary, as such, but it looked healthy and powerful. I wanted to get away from it as quietly as I could, but my feet were heavy and stuck to the spot.

Its ears twitched and it suddenly stopped nosing the ground; my heart raced. It looked directly at me, and the intelligence in its dark eyes was somehow more terrifying than if it had attacked me on sight.

Why are you here? A voice, somehow distinct from my own thoughts, penetrated my mind. My mouth wouldn't open to respond. The voice repeated, firmly: **Why are you here?**

"I- I'm sorry," I whispered.

What do you want?

"What do I- uh, what do I want? I'm sorry." Internally, I was cowering, but my body stayed stock-still. It was a miracle I was talking at all. After the initial shock, though, it was beginning to feel normal to hear the dog speak to me like this.

You've come here for some reason, surely. I can help you, but only if you tell me what you want.

"Anything?"

Only if you tell me what you want. The dog yawned; I guess this back and forth was boring it.

"I want my wife back. Just before she died. I want her back like she was before she died."

The dog blinked slowly at me. It seemed pensive somehow. **As you wish.**

It walked away, tail down. I felt untethered from where I stood, at last, but my knees were weak and wobbly and I fell onto the grass.

I was awoken the next morning by the sun coming through the curtains. I mustn't have shut them properly the night before - it'd been a long week, and I was exhausted. Toasty nestled in his favourite spot on my bed, and he looked straight into my eyes when I opened them. His paw stretched out onto my leg and he butted my leg affectionately. I made a note of my dream before I forgot.

I rolled onto the empty side of the bed and got up to go to the bathroom. Toasty protested loudly.

"I know! I know!" I said to him. "Yes, meow, meow!"

Strangely, the bathroom door was shut. I'd had some windows open, so it must have been wind currents slamming it shut.

I noticed a slip of paper tucked under the door, and I felt like I lost control of my body. That awful sensation in my legs I felt in the dream returned, and I fell to my knees. My hands trembled as I unfolded the paper.

I'm sorry
- S

"No... no, no, that's not..." I heard my voice. I had never been able to bring myself to look at the note she'd left five years ago, but the handwriting was unmistakeable, and it was written on one of the sticky notes we'd had at the time that had long since run out.

I stood up and pushed open the door, and heard soft breaths catching in a throat. I kept my eyes on the floor, but I knew what was there. I steeled myself and lifted my head.

She was there again. Her left arm, hooked over the rim of the bath, was steadily seeping blood onto the floor. She turned her head to look at me weakly.

"Mark?" she murmured.

I ran to kneel on the floor next to her. My trembling wouldn't subside. "Serena? It's me, it's okay, I'm here," I tried to reassure her.

"It's too late," Serena said. "I'm sorry."

I picked up her hand and she winced. I moved my hands to caress her face and shakily smeared blood onto her hair and cheek. I wanted to cry, but I was beyond that point. Her eyes were watering.

The water in the bath was dark and reeked of meat and iron.

"Why?" I pleaded, searching her fading face for answers.

She shook her head like a child. "I'm sorry," was all she said.

I sat with her, leaning my head gently on her shoulder as she bled, and listened to her shallow breaths. I didn't know if my presence made her feel better or worse. I told her I loved her, but her only response was to apologise.

It felt like a lifetime that I spent with her there, sitting on the cold floor, her warm blood slowly pooling and soaking into my clothes. After she drew her final breath, I sat with her for some time after, looking at her, stroking her hair.

The wounds in her arms were desperate and deep, and more criss-crossed her legs. The arm exposed to air was half-covered in a crimson-black crust by the time I left the bathroom, and the bathwater was beginning to separate into solidified blood and clear water. I kissed her cheek and stared at the half-closed eyes that had haunted my memories for years.

I returned to my bedroom feeling like I could never feel anything again. Toasty fled at the sight of me shaking and covered in Serena's blood, and somehow, that made the floodgates burst open: I sobbed.

I spent nearly all day in place. Somehow, my mind felt empty and yet full of panicky thoughts. For one, how does one deal with the corpse of somebody buried years before?

In the backyard, I had a small shed, mostly used as extra storage. I pulled on shoes and ran outside in my pyjama trousers, throwing the door open. As I remembered: it had a wooden floor I could pull up, and there was only soil underneath.

Suddenly aware of how strange it would look if I was caught pulling up the floorboards, I shut the shed door. Was it suspicious to be in the shed for a long time? Which would be more suspicious? I knew, really, that it was unlikely anyone would notice, let alone care, but I felt hypersensitive to any shift or noise. As I worked, a police siren sounded in the distance, and I crouched, covering my head, until it was out of earshot.

There was a foot or so gap between the floor and the ground, and so I dug deeper, piling the soil to the side of the shed furthest from the door. I moved quickly back into the house and up to the bathroom.

The room stank, and the metallic scent was spilling into the corridor. I drained the bath. The water had left the flesh around her wounds white and slightly swollen, and the hand she'd had submerged had wrinkled grotesquely.

By this point in the day, I knew there was little time left where I'd have sunlight, and there were no lights in the shed. I picked up some old bed linen that had gone unused for ages and dropped it near the bath. I tried to pick up Serena's body, but it seemed impossible to grab her anywhere that wasn't slit. I ran to the toilet and vomited.

Instead, I gently draped a sheet over her, like the corpses in autopsy rooms in television shows. The cotton clung to her nose, chin, breasts, and thighs from residual water. With her body covered up, I picked her up, placed her on the floor, and rolled her up, first in the sheet, and again in a duvet cover. The floor, the sheets, and I were smeared in watered-down blood, and I covered myself in a coat before I carried the body over my shoulder into the shed. Running would look more suspicious: I tried to look as casual as I could.

When the soil was patted down, I left the floorboards for the day due to the waning sunlight, although the near-impossible chance that someone might look in the shed and suspect something was driving me completely mad.

I tried to get my head around what had happened.

It was the dog from my dreams, wasn't it? It had to have been. Unless I had never woken up, and I was due to wake up for real anytime now...

I was still shaking, and a pain in my stomach reminded me that I hadn't eaten all day. I didn't have any appetite. I forced down a bowl of cereal and noticed blood under my nails.

All else that remained of Serena in my house was the bloodied bathroom, which I cleaned in a strange stupor. I showered, and the water falling on me felt vague, yet stabbing. I thought of the blood I'd cleaned. I thought of the sensation of the wounds in her skin, and nearly threw up again at the memory. I thought of my beautiful wife sleeping underground in my shed.

I didn't expect to sleep that night, but I was exhausted emotionally, mentally, physically. I'd dropped the suicide note by my bedroom door in the day. Now, I picked it up and held it tightly in my fist, over my heart.

I was in the same field as before. The sky was yellow-ish grey and the heat was unbearable. The breeze that blew the white rows of seeds in the long grass brought no respite from the suffocating blanket of warmth. I saw it: the same dog! the horrible creature that did this to me!

I didn't wait for it to notice me this time. "What did you do?" I yelled, the previous night's fear gone.

The dog blinked and panted, looking at me. **I did as you asked.**

"As I-?" I was incredulous, but paused for a second. "Oh, for fuck's sake. 'Just before she died'. That's what I said, wasn't it?"

That is what you said. That is what you wished for.

I held my head in my hands. "That is what I wished for. Right. Oh, god, oh god oh god oh god." The dog looked into the distance. "Do I get more wishes? What is this, a three-wishes type deal?"

It looked back at me. I felt pitied, and I hated it.

"Do I get more wishes? Answer me!"

I did as you asked. What more could you want?

I knelt down and clasped my hands together, pleading. There was blood under my nails. "Please... let me try again. I beg you."

You don't need to beg. What do you want?

"Can you bring her back and stop her feeling that...

that pain?”

I don’t have the ability to manipulate the emotions of humans. That would be a violation of free will.

“Just... I want my wife alive,” I tried to collect myself. “I would like my wife to be as she was... the day before she died, yes. And if she does the same thing again... I don’t know, I just want her back. I don’t want to wake up in my bed without her there, alive and well, ever again.”

The dog pawed at the ground for a second, disinterested. **As you wish.**

The dream jolted me awake early, but something was different. A certain weight I wasn't used to in the bed, a presence too big to be Toasty. In the grey half-light, I saw a shape in bed next to me: a slim figure, facing away from me and curled in the foetal position. I sat up sharply. She turned at my movement, rubbing an eye with a clumsy hand.

"Ughh... what is it?"

"Serena!" I cried out, and kissed her.

"What? What's got into you?" she murmured, but she turned to face me, and I wrapped my arms around her. For the first time in years, I slept holding my wife.

In the morning, I thought about asking her about her suicide. Did she remember it? Did she still want to kill herself? I slipped the note I'd grasped in the night into my dream diary and shook the thoughts from my mind for the time being.

She slept longer than I did, like she used to. I caressed her cheek and crept out of bed. I couldn't stop smiling! I felt like a child on Christmas. Serena was there! She was real and alive and as beautiful as she ever was. I cooked her bacon and scrambled eggs - the bacon crispy, the eggs a little bit more liquid, as she liked - and I brought them up to our bedroom, where she sat up sleepily.

"Oh! Thank you!" She accepted the plate, and I sat on the edge of the bed, admiring her. "What's gotten into you? What's the occasion?" she asked, looking at me strangely. She gasped abruptly: "Wait, why didn't the alarm for work go off?"

"It's Sunday, and I love you. Is that so wrong?"

"Oh!" she laughed uncertainly. "Well, I love you too. I could have sworn it was a Thursday. Look at me, losing track of the days!" She reached over, careful not to let her food slide off her plate, and squeezed my hand.

When she had eaten, she slipped out of bed towards the bathroom, and my stomach dropped briefly.

"Mark?" she called out.

"Yeah?"

"Where's my shampoo? Where's my bath stuff?" She re-entered the bedroom, looking confused. Damn it! I hadn't considered any of this.

"Uh, I guess you must have run out," I tried to act as nonchalant as I could.

"Run out of everything? And just didn't notice before? That doesn't make any sense!"

"I guess not..." I responded weakly. "Just use my stuff and we'll go shopping later." Serena didn't seem any less confused, but she nodded.

This was bad. I took her plate downstairs, and took the opportunity to pull down the calendar in the hallway and anything else I could see that might bring up uncomfortable questions, but there was no way she wasn't going to see something was off at some point...

After her shower, she asked after her phone. I could see this was going to be a real thorn in my side.

"Oh, yeah. You dropped it and it died the other day, didn't it?" I lied, thinking quickly. She didn't look convinced.

"Did it? Oh... Hey, your phone looks really different. When did you get a new one?"

I decided to make a day of our little shopping trip. I led Serena, as subtly as I could, to the weird back-alley shops I thought she'd like best, acting as though it was my first time seeing them, as though she'd discovered them herself. I felt so honoured to be standing by her, drinking in her happiness like it was ambrosia. She seemed a little distracted, though, and I couldn't shake the nervousness that that instilled in me.

"Huh. I don't remember that Starbucks. I thought that was the butcher's?" she wondered aloud.

"Ah, yeah. Must have been taken over recently," I lied.

"When did that big supermarket open up?"

"Oh, is that statue new? It looks like it's been there for a while, but I swear I've never seen it before..."

Her questions were constant, and I had no answers for any of them. I wished I'd made an excuse to leave her at home.

We sat inside a cafe - one that she had liked before she died - and she stared at me suspiciously with her lovely sky-blue eyes.

"It feels like... I've been asleep for a long time," she said.

I swallowed and stared at my cappuccino. "Oh, yeah?"

"I swear things have changed overnight. Am I going mad?" She laughed, but there was a manic edge to it that worried me.

"Of course not, love! You're fine," I clasped my hands around hers and looked her deep in her eyes. "Sometimes, you just don't notice little things. Maybe you've been stressed and it's made you forgetful."

When we got home, shopping bags in tow, we watched television curled up on the sofa together. It felt like no time had passed at all, and I flicked through channels nonchalantly when the news or any other reminder of the date came up, almost as much for my own sake as Serena's. It was much nicer to pretend the time without her had never happened. She fell asleep, and I stroked her hair gently. I remembered how, not long ago, I was caressing the face of her corpse in the same way. In the corners of my fingernails, there were still traces of her blood. I shuddered, and tried to put it out of my mind.

I took her out for dinner that evening, somewhere she'd begged to try for a long time, but which I always refused because it seemed horribly overpriced. Well, I didn't care about price now, not if it made Serena happy.

That same damned expression was on her face, though. She looked so beautiful - I was grateful now that I'd never had the heart to get rid of her clothes, and I'd gently prompted her to buy some nice new makeup, my treat, earlier that day - but still, I couldn't stand that wary way she was looking at me.

"If we weren't married, I'd think you were planning on proposing," she joked, that tense note still in her voice.

"Can't I treat you sometimes?" I said.

"I guess so. It's been a lovely day," Her eyes dropped down to her plate of seafood pasta, which she was pushing around her plate. "The food's nice. I told you, Marie said it was good."

Marie? I hadn't heard from her since Serena's funeral. They'd worked together, I think.

Wait a second: what if someone we knew saw us? How would I explain Serena's presence to them? How would I explain their shock to Serena? Shit. I tried to peer around as inconspicuously as possible. I couldn't see anyone I recognised, but I couldn't look around too well with Serena sat facing me, either.

"You've been acting weird today," Serena said, brow furrowed.

"Oh, have I? Sorry." She opened her mouth to speak, but I signalled a waiter and ordered more wine before she had a chance to continue.

The rest of the dinner was eaten in relative silence, bar some small talk about the food and the wine. When I wasn't looking at her, I felt Serena's eyes burning into me; when I looked up, she'd go back to prodding her food as though she hadn't been staring.

We went to bed straight away when we returned home, and Serena was laying on her back, head on her arms, staring at the ceiling.

"What are you thinking about?" I asked.

"Ah... I don't know." She went quiet, considering something for a while. "Thanks for everything today, though," she said, touching my arm affectionately. Her smile disappeared as soon as her eyes lost contact with mine, and she turned away from me.

"Are you okay?" I asked, grasping her shoulder.

She turned her head, and I saw her mouth open and close a few times, trying to gather whatever words she wanted to say, and failing. Eventually, she sighed. "Yeah, it's fine."

I shrugged. "Okay, good." Settling down in bed, I ran my fingers along her side. Even in the simple nightdresses she wore, she was stunning. I cuddled up to her, kissing her neck, and she tensed up under my touch.

"Mark... no, I want to sleep," she said, shuffling away from me.

"You always say that."

"Well, it's true!"

"Then maybe you shouldn't be so beautiful," I smiled into her ear, craning my neck to kiss her cheek and wrapping my arm around her.

"You're so corny sometimes," she laughed, but her body was still tense. As much as I loved her, I hated how hard it could be to seduce her.

I knew how to get through to her, though.

Afterwards, I felt a completeness that I hadn't felt for years, something that my favourite sex worker was never able to stir in me. Nothing could compare to Serena, and I was almost driven to tears at the sheer thought of how lucky I was to experience her body again.

When I came back to bed after cleaning myself up, I saw that Serena had resumed staring at the ceiling. She didn't seem to notice when I turned off the light.

In the morning, when my alarm went off for work, I was hit with the realisation that she would be expecting to work today, too; the sentiment was a rude awakening from the cosy happiness of waking up next to my wife.

She was stirring: we had both worked 9-5 jobs. As she stretched and rubbed her eyes, I feigned tender concern.

"Oh, honey, look at you! Are you feeling okay?" I reached out to touch her forehead.

"I'm tired, but I think I'm okay," Serena sat up, yawning. "Why, do I look sick?"

"Are you sure? I swear your forehead's hot."

"It's warm in here. I feel just fine."

I shook my head and sighed, hoping I wasn't laying it on too thick as I did so. "Well, you don't want to bring anything into work, do you? Maybe you're just starting to come down with something and you'll feel it more in a bit. Imagine getting stuck at work when that happens!"

"Then I'll just go home. My boss isn't a complete monster," Serena frowned, leaning on one arm. "I feel fine. I can't look that bad, surely."

"I mean, it's your choice," I raised my hands. She was growing more uncertain, at least. "I would phone in sick, if I were you. Ah, you don't have a phone! I know the number for your work. I'll call them for you."

"Wh- no, wait!" Serena was bemused as I turned away, pretending to find the number on my phone.

"Hello," I said to nobody. "Yes, this is Mark, Serena's husband. Hello, yeah, she's not feeling so well today so she won't be in." I paused, nodding. "I'm sure she'll be fine soon. I'll let her know you said that. Okay, bye!" I prodded my screen to hang up.

Serena had her mouth slightly open and her brow furrowed; her eyes bore into me. Her hands were clenching the sheets, and I was scared I'd gone too far, but she took some deep breaths and whispered, "Okay."

I stroked her hair and kissed her forehead. "You're so stubborn sometimes. I can't watch you overdo it if you're coming down with something! I did it for your own good. You know that."

She laid back down, silent for a moment. "I guess things have been a bit... like it lately. Maybe you're right," she murmured eventually.

I checked on her before I left for work, and told her I loved her. I didn't know how I was going to keep up this façade.

When I returned home, I was greeted with an altogether different Serena to the one I'd left huddled up in bed. She was smiling and chatty, flitting around the kitchen to finish up cooking something.

"Oh! Are you making bolognese?" I asked.

"Yeah! To thank you for yesterday. I know it's not much, but it's your favourite, isn't it? So I thought it'd be nice, maybe..."

"You don't need to explain yourself," I wrapped my arms around her from behind and kissed her cheek. "Where did the ingredients come from? I don't remember buying mince or mushrooms yesterday."

Serena looked at me incredulously. "The shop, silly! Oh, you won't believe who I saw. Robert and Sarah! I didn't get the chance to say hello, but I haven't seen them since Lyn's birthday party, when was it, last year? Maybe two years ago now, actually. They looked like they'd seen a ghost! I know I got a bit drunk, but I hope I didn't offend them or something..." She stirred the pasta and lowered her voice a little. "Although, I have to say, they've aged more than I expected since I last saw them; they're not looking good at all." She craned her neck to look at me. "Do you look older? Do we look that much older than back then? Maybe I just don't notice the changes so much because we see each other all the time. Isn't that weird?"

I was staring at nothing in particular, hoping to God that the pound of my heartbeat wasn't loud enough for Serena to hear. I faked a quick laugh. "Yeah, weird. But you really shouldn't be going out when you're unwell."

I was happy, at least, to see Serena in high spirits. She chattered throughout dinner. What a contrast to the silence in the house for the past few years! She pointed out a picture I'd put up near the dining table of a family on a beach somewhere, maybe sometime in the '80s.

"Who are they? I don't recognise that picture."

"I got it at some charity shop, I think," I said.

"Oh! That's so sad. It's sweet that you decided to give them a home with us!" She squinted in thought at the photo for a minute, and started to make up personalities and backstories for them all.

"Look at all that chest hair on the dad! He was probably a looker when he was younger, but now he just sits and complains to his son about how men were *men* back in *his* day..." she twittered, her hands illustrating the pictures she described. "Now, *she* always wanted to make it as a fashion designer - look at that swimsuit, isn't it fantastic? But it never worked out, because... hmmm..."

I listened, and smiled.

Toasty wandered into the kitchen; he was usually fed around my dinnertime. It occurred to me he hadn't been sleeping on the bed now that Serena was back.

"Hello, Toasty!" Serena called, making kissy noises and wiggling her fingers at him. His hackles raised, and he crept back out, looking towards her nervously. She sighed, and looked as sad as she had that morning for just a moment. "He's been so off with me the past couple of days. I must have done something to slight him. Cats, huh?" She smiled. I was glad that Toasty couldn't speak.

Before bed, I caught Serena staring at her face closely in the mirror. She looked sheepish when she saw me standing in the door to the bathroom.

"Sorry. Thinking about aging again. Maybe I do look old. I've been feeling old lately. Tired, you know."

"Well, you're still the prettiest girl I've ever seen," I said, tucking her hair behind her ear and going in for a kiss. She turned to offer me her cheek, and I caught her on the lips as she pulled away.

At work the next day, I couldn't focus on anything. All I could think about was her: my thoughts fluctuated between ecstacy at her return to my life and fear that she'd be discovered by somebody else.

"Mark?" David, my manager, approached my desk, placing his hands down forcefully.

"Yes? Is everything okay?"

"Where's the report? It was meant to be done by midday."

I stared at my screen blankly.

"Look, you're in the position you're in because you're competent. This isn't like you. Don't let it happen again, okay? And get that report sent over within the hour," David looked at me pointedly, and walked away before I could respond.

The text on my screen swam in front of my eyes. I hadn't been scolded like that for years, and I scrambled to get ahold of myself.

As I unlocked the front door, I heard gentle music playing. A wave of relief flowed through me. I walked upstairs as quietly as I could, and stood for a while, listening to Serena's viola. I had a whole new appreciation for the soulful, yearning song that she could draw from the strings. When she paused, I opened the door, and she jumped slightly.

"Hello! Good day at work?"

I nodded. "Keep playing."

"Oh!" She smiled nervously. "Okay, then."

I sat on the bed, and she played, glancing at me and giggling girlishly between pieces. Her sweetness made my heart feel full.

At dinner, she was quiet, as though thinking. I didn't want to interrupt her.

"Thank you for listening to me," she murmured, and I jumped at the broken silence.

"Hmm? Oh, of course. I like listening to you play."

She tilted her head and gazed at me, as through prying into my mind. I felt my cheeks flush, vulnerable under her eyes.

"Good," she said. After a few more minutes of silence, "You know, I've been wanting a break from work for the longest time, but now it's only been two days and I'm already so bored. I'll never be happy, will I?"

Her tone was jovial, but her words unsettled me a little, nonetheless, and the atmosphere seemed to shift, growing colder.

In the morning, she saw me off from work smiling, but something in the wideness of her eyes made me feel the same chill.

Maybe that's why my heart sank when I returned home to Toasty crying loudly, and why I felt strangely unsurprised to see Serena in the bath for the third time.

She was positioned a bit differently, but she had opted for the same method. I supposed that made sense: it must have been something she'd been planning for a while.

Another slip of paper. As before:

I'm sorry
- S

I knelt on the floor, head resting on the side of the bath, crumpling the note in my hand. Again?

I found another old, faded set of bed linen and wrapped her corpse methodically, if shakily, and bridal carried her body down the stairs and into the shed. It seemed as though I was watching myself from an outside perspective as I dug up some of the ground in the shed, stopping when I felt my shovel hit the corpse I'd buried previously, and laid her to rest again.

Was this going to keep happening? What was I doing wrong, that she still felt she had no option but to die?

I cleaned the bathroom and myself again. I hadn't changed out of my work clothes, I realised, and had bloodied my shirt. I made a mental note to look up how to get blood out of fabric.

I stared into the horizon, with its endless grey-yellow clouds, and felt like crying.

I didn't expect to see you again so soon.

I looked down at the grass and saw that same dog again. I willed myself to wake up.

You're becoming quite the frequent guest.

That pissed me off. "You- you scammed me!"

"Scammed"? What a strange accusation.

The heat was becoming enough that it was hard to breathe, the air felt so heavy and humid. I wondered idly how the dog dealt with the heat with its thick black fur. My stupid outburst was all I could muster. I didn't have it in me to argue.

Your wish isn't over yet.

"Mark? Mark!" Serena was nudging me.

Wait.

"Serena? What the fuck is going on?" I must still be dreaming.

"I had an awful nightmare." She felt too real, too soft, too warm, even for my vivid dreams. "I dreamt I... I dreamt I bled to death."

I started and sat up, staring at her in the grey half-light. "What?"

"It felt so real... I really felt like that's how it is to die," she continued. "It was scary, but..."

She cuddled up to me. I held her close, and I soon felt her breathing become slow and calm. There was blood under my nails.

I lay awake until my alarm went off for work.

Serena clung to me as I started to stir.

"Are you okay, love?" I asked. I was feeling the shock of seeing her dead again more now than I was last night.

Her fingers clenched, gripping my shoulders with a strength unexpected of her delicate hands. "Just... a bit shaken. I'll be okay."

"Dreams can be tough, huh?" I said sincerely. I knew all too well the horrors that dreams can conjure.

"Sorry, you need to get ready for work, don't you?"

Her grip on me loosened, and she laid back, staring at the ceiling. She was pale: the dark circles under her eyes and the blue of her veins snaking through her inner arms contrasted against her white skin as though she were carved from marble. Even fearful and exhausted, she was art to me.

I stroked her cheek with my thumb affectionately and pulled a grim attempt at a smile.

She lasted a few days - a few beautiful days - before I came home to her body hanging from the banister by some cables knotted together. I was grateful not to deal with blood again. Toasty had pissed in the corner of the hallway.

The night before, she'd turned to me in bed before we slept, and pondered, "Do you think it really feels scary to die? Or is it less scary than it seems? Maybe it's just like sleep."

"You're tired. Stop talking nonsense," I tried to make my tone light-hearted, but my jaw had clenched and I spoke through gritted teeth.

"Sorry," she murmured. "Just thinking out loud."

I grunted in response. I'd been trying to make her happy. I'd been cooking for her, ordering her gifts, bringing home her favourite wines to drink with dinner, but she always stared blankly at the luxuries I presented her with, and her eventual thanks always rang too hollow.

"What did I do wrong this time?" I snapped at Serena's hanging body. Her mouth was slightly open, as though she was wondering what to say. "What was it? What's the problem? Why do you keep doing... this?" I slammed my fist down on the side table, keys in hand, knocking off a tacky ceramic duck and jamming the back door key into the heel of my hand.

About three quarters of the duck's head stared up at me piteously as blood - my blood, for once - dripped onto the welcome mat. I'd bought it a few years ago because it looked like something Serena would find cute. I'd been right.

"What did I do wrong this time?" I repeated to myself, my eyes welling up.

I didn't have any more expendable linen. I draped a blanket over her corpse, sat her in a corner of the shed as I scraped another hollow into the dirt, and dropped her in unceremoniously. Back in the house, I threw the blanket into the laundry basket, sat down, and cried.

I awoke in the morning to Serena sleeping fitfully. I watched her, pondering whether it was better or worse to wake her up. Maybe all of my efforts to make her happy were futile. Maybe it was some sort of fate thing that meant she had to kill herself. Maybe, even if I was the perfect husband, she'd be hit by a car tragically, or fall terminally ill, because that was just how things were.

Serena was making distressed squeaks. I laid a hand on her cheek gently, and she slowly blinked awake.

"I died again..." she choked. My eyes felt swollen and sore from crying, and they stung as they welled up again. "It's so scary," she continued, and I kissed her.

"How can I make you happy?" I blurted.

"What?" Serena frowned. "Right now, I just want a decent night's sleep, to be honest."

And so the cycle went: Serena would wake up next to me no matter what happened. I would get a few days with her before she had one of her "nightmares", which were even more horrible for me.

When I returned home to the smell of food cooking, or the sound of the viola, my heart would soar. When it was quiet - or, worse, when Toasty was crying - my stomach would drop and I'd steel myself for what I might find. Sometimes, she was napping on the sofa, long eyelashes fluttering when she sensed my presence, or reading peacefully, and I'd sigh in relief and hug her.

Sometimes, I wasn't so lucky.

There she was, pill packets strewn around her, laid back in bed, but too cold to be sleeping. There she was, bent over on the kitchen floor, her stomach split, her hands still clenched around the kitchen knife. I once caught Toasty sniffing around cautiously, lapping up some of the blood, and he looked at me guiltily when he saw me watching. Hanging from the banister again. Bled out in the bath again. Overdosed again.

I found solace in the knowledge that she'd be there again in the morning, but working every day, not knowing whether or not I'd have a body to bury later on, was draining in every sense.

Sometimes, I wondered if it was hurting her, keeping her alive like this.

"Am I real?" she said at dinner one evening.

"Of course you are."

"I don't feel real anymore. I can't tell when I'm awake and when I'm dreaming," Serena's laugh, which usually brought me such joy, stang with jagged hysteria. "I don't know if I feel at all anymore!"

She stopped eating, no matter what I prepared for her or ordered in.

"What can I do to make you happy?" I asked from time to time.

"Why do you keep asking me that?"

"It hurts to see you like this."

"It hurts you, does it?" Again, that horrible laugh. "I bet it does."

"Well, I want you to be happy," I said, dolefully.

"I don't think..." Serena looked at me, and I couldn't fathom at all what her expression meant. "It's not your responsibility. It's okay. I'm sure I'll get better."

She haunted the house like a shadow. The only life left in her that I ever witnessed was when she played viola, its deep song resonating through the house. She slept either totally still, and I'd put my hand to her nose to check she was breathing; or struggling, crying, and choking.

In my dreams, I sometimes saw the strange dog in the distance, or glimpsed it lurking somewhere nearby. I wondered if it was checking up on me.

As Serena had died again and again, I had become lax in how I dealt with the bodies. The shed's floor never got put back down, and I had nigh-on given up on making sure the corpses were covered in more than a thin layer of dirt. It seemed pointless to be thorough: inevitably, there'd be another body to bury.

Still, I should have paid more attention.
I came home to the house silent, as though filled with fog, and started when I heard a sigh.

Cautiously, I entered the living room. Serena was sat on the sofa, staring down at her cupped hands.

"Hello, love. How's your day been?" I said.

Serena said nothing. I leant over to look at what she was holding, and she shied away from me. It was her watch - a delicate gold thing that she'd received before we'd even met.

"What's wrong?" I reached out towards her, and she squeaked quietly as she dodged me. It was then that I realised my mistake.

I was always so careful to take off any jewellery she had on when I cleaned up her bodies! How did I miss that? Stupid, stupid, stupid...

I clenched my jaw. I couldn't let on that I'd been caught, because then what? "Is there something wrong with your watch?" I squatted down and tried to make eye contact with her. "Hey. Look at me."

She sat still, her stare directed unfaltering at the watch. Tears glistened in her eyes, and her tense body seemed brittle, fragile. "Why was this in the shed, Mark?" she said, finally. Her words were quiet, but deep with rage.

"The shed? I don't know. How strange!" My voice came out strained and breathy.

"Do you know what else was in the shed, Mark?" She turned her face to me, stony, even streaked with tears.

I floundered, my mouth hanging open for a second.

"N-no? Tools, maybe?"

Serena pursed her lips. "Not even going to try to lie, huh." She looked back down at her watch.

"What were you doing in the shed, anyway?" I asked as authoritatively as I could muster.

She looked shocked. "Does it really matter when I found..." Her eyes closed. "You're lucky I didn't call the police immediately."

"You think they'll believe you?" I spoke without thinking.

Serena glared at me hatefully, and ran, suddenly, to the landline in the kitchen. I chased after her: she'd picked up the phone and had started pressing buttons. I heard the dial tone, and grasped the handset, scrambling to hang up. She started trying to redial, and, desperately, I wrapped my arm around her neck and tried to pry the phone from her fingers. She bit down on my wrist and I reflexively shoved her away.

The phone landed on the floor, random numbers on the little screen. I heard Serena crash heavily into something, but she didn't cry out.

"I'm sorry... I'm so sorry. Serena? Hey, Serena?" I rushed to her side, and her body was limp and heavy as I turned her over. Blood was slowly seeping from her temple into her hairline.

What were the fucking chances, I thought. She must have hit the counter badly.

Dusk had fallen by the time I went out to the shed as quietly as possible. The paranoia I had felt when I buried my first body had long since waned to nothing, but now I was feeling hypervigilant all over again. I needed a torch to light the space within the shed, and I imagined a neighbour looking out the window or the police knocking on the door or God knows what...

From what I could see, Serena had scraped at some dirt that barely covered a body, and increasingly deep and frantic claw marks in the dirt were still visible from where she'd dug deeper, exposing parts of more corpses. I placed the newest body into the ground, and quietly, carefully, I pushed soil back over the pile. I put down the floorboards that had been leaning against a wall, out of the way. Prying them up had been far easier than putting them back, as it turned out, and I cringed at every knock and creak that I made. They didn't need to be secure - in fact, that'd be worse, because there was sure to be a new body to bury soon - but they had to be sound enough to quell any suspicions. The key was going to stay with me at all times from now on, I knew that for sure.

I tried to reason with myself about this death. She would have died anyway, so was it really so bad if this one was my fault? It certainly felt worse, but that was me being emotional, surely. Maybe, because it was me who killed her, and not another suicide, this would be the end of it. Was that a good thing? Was I happier before I brought her back? I felt like I was destined to be miserable, either way.

I woke to only Toasty on my bed, and felt that conflict all over again. When I went downstairs for breakfast, though, Serena was sat at the dining table, head in her heads.

"Good morning, beautiful," I said, sitting next to her.

She said nothing.

"Are you okay? You were upset yesterday," I prompted.

She turned her head towards me briefly and set it back into her hands with a resigned sigh. Her watch caught the light on her delicate wrist.

"Please talk to me," I laid a hand on her shoulder, which she shook off quickly. "I want to help."

"They were all me," she spat after an eternity. "So many of them. In the shed. What the FUCK?" Her voice raised to a yell at the end, and she started sobbing.

"What are you talking about?"

"Don't play dumb. There are bodies in the shed, Mark. How do you explain that?"

"You were dreaming, I'm sure. You've been having weird dreams, haven't you?" I stooped down and tried to put my arms around her.

"Get off me! Get the fuck away from me! You killed me, I know it!" she cried, batting my arms away, her face red and screwed-up like a child throwing a tantrum. Language like that felt so wrong in her voice, usually high-pitched and gentle.

"Please, Serena," I tried to keep myself composed. "Come on. Let's look in the shed together, okay?" I gripped her shoulder, resisting her shakes this time. "Let's go, okay?"

Sobs racked her shoulders for some time, until, eventually, she sighed deeply. "Okay," she whispered, sniffling. "But don't fucking touch me."

I led her to the shed, and she went pale as I pushed the

door open. Inside, it was normal: dusty, messy, and containing no visible corpses. There was a strange, lingering smell, but I reassured myself that I was only really noticing it because I knew its source. I was working hard to keep my breathing steady: I was relieved to see it look so inconspicuous, myself.

"But-" Serena began.

"See? It's fine. You had a bad dream. It's okay. I know they feel real sometimes," I gently, but firmly, interrupted her.

"They were right here... the floor was gone. Take up the floor! Take it up, they're there!" she begged shrilly.

"Come on, don't be silly. It was obviously a dream. The shed looks the same as it ever does. You never even *go* to the shed."

"Yeah..." Serena blinked hard. "Yeah, I guess." She fell into my arms heavily, and I held her close.

"You're safe, I promise," I said, kissing her head. "I love you. You know I'd never hurt you. It's all just a bad dream."

A few days later, I woke up to an empty bed, and found her hanging in my wardrobe. Somehow, although clearing up corpses was becoming pretty normal to me, I couldn't stop the images of her dead bodies from invading my vision whenever I closed my eyes.

With no real friends, any socialising I did was at work, but that was becoming impossible now. It felt as though, if I were to even begin to speak of anything outside work, everything I was hiding would spill out, and I would talk about nothing but cold flesh and congealed pools of blood and the glassy eyes of the woman I loved more than anything...

No, I had to keep it to myself. If workplace small talk had to be ruled out, that was fine.

Sometimes, I thought about the various ways Serena had died. I wondered which hurt most, which killed fastest, which was the quickest escape.

Sometimes, those thoughts were the only interludes I had to the grotesque slideshow of death my mind played on a loop.

"Am I dead?" Serena asked me abruptly one day when I returned from work.

"What? You're here right now, aren't you?"

"There was something I saw... I read your dream diary. There was weird stuff in there." Her eyes wouldn't meet me, and her voice shook a little.

"You- that's private, when did I say you could read that?" My words were high-pitched in my panic. "You can't just look at my stuff!"

"I didn't mean to! I promise," she looked up at me wide-eyed. "I was looking for a notebook to write something down, and it was the first one I found. I didn't mean to, I swear! But there were these notes, and-"

"You shouldn't have read what was on the page! What's wrong with you?" I raised my hand, but I couldn't bring myself to strike her.

Serena shrank beneath me and her eyes began to

water. "I'm sorry, I'm sorry."

I'd gone too far. I embraced her. "I've been having weird dreams, too. That's all."

The next time she died - hanging again, which, with how often she did it, I guessed was her preference - I noticed blood on the outer thigh of her jeans. When I looked at her hand, I realised she'd cut off her fingers.

She'd hastily wrapped the mutilated hand in tissues, which I picked off to inspect the stumps. As I pondered the bloodied palm, I heard the pit-pat of Toasty walking nearby.

He paused and looked at me guiltily: he was holding something in his mouth.

"Hey, what have you got?" I let Serena's hand fall and walked towards him. I put my hand out. "Come on, Toasty, what have you got?" My voice quavered as I held him by the scruff and tried to pull what he was holding from his mouth. He struggled, and his sharp teeth scraped me, but I grabbed it.

As Toasty ran off to huff and clean himself indignantly, I confirmed what I'd already known: he'd found one of the fingers before I even had a chance to search for them. It was stiff and curled up, and the cut end was ragged. It must have hurt like hell. Why would she go to this much trouble?

Toasty was off with me the rest of the evening, although I left the finger for him to chew on, if he really wanted.

The next day, Serena confronted me with another of the severed fingers.

"I knew it," she said, holding the finger out to me.

"What?"

"I knew it," she repeated. "I've been dying. You lied to me."

"Then why are you here now?" It was the only argument I had.

"You expect me to know? What I *do* know is that this is my finger, and I bet I know where more of them are."

"You... hid fingers around the house?" I was incredulous. She'd been proving a theory! There wasn't any way I could wriggle out of this one.

"Does it really matter what I did? You've much more to explain than I do."

"Let me see your hands," I demanded. She complied. As I expected, they were perfectly intact.

I sighed and took the severed finger from her. I couldn't say it wasn't her finger, because who else would it belong to? "Convincing fake," I said eventually. "How'd you find someone to make that?"

"Ugh!" Serena flounced off somewhere. I found her, later, in the spare room, curled up with an empty bottle of whisky and pill packets. I sighed. It was only the cheap whisky, at least, but I'd just restocked on painkillers.

After that confrontation, she seemed to be killing herself more out of spite than anything else.

On the occasions that Serena lasted more than a day,

she would sleep in the spare room. On mornings following a death, I'd wake up as early as I could to spend some time with her, watching her sleep. Despite everything, I still loved her, but it was only when she was sleeping that there was peace between us.

Often, when she did wake up next to me, she would tell me, matter-of-factly, how she felt like dying that day.

"Please don't speak like that," I'd beg her.

"I'm only giving you fair warning," she'd shrug.

It had to be said, sometimes she didn't give me that courtesy. Sometimes, she'd get out of bed and string herself up immediately, without a single word. As dull as I was becoming to grief, my heart would ache all day when she did something like that. I'd kiss her cold cheek goodbye and deal with the mess when I returned from work. Worse was when she'd time the more violent deaths, it seemed, so that I'd enter the room just as she plunged a kitchen knife into her chest, or slit the arteries in her neck. Her eyes would meet mine, hateful and sad, and I'd feel like it was my flesh the blade was splitting.

One Saturday morning, I woke up to her staring at me.

"Hmm?" I murmured.

"Maybe all this has been a bad dream," she said, expressionless. "But then why do I feel everything like it's real?"

I was still half-asleep and not up to these questions. "Does it matter?"

I felt similarly, but telling her so would seem strangely

like defeat.

Awkwardly, Serena shifted up to me and embraced me.

"I still love you," she whispered. I kissed her, and for the first time in a long time, she didn't resist me. When she laid her head on my chest, I felt her tears soak through my T-shirt. "I don't know what's real anymore. But I... I think I still love you."

It seemed that that was the end of that. A truce, somehow, had been called. Serena began to act more like her usual self over the next few days. She was laughing, and cooking, and we were cuddling on the sofa with glasses of wine.

She began to spend the night in my bed again of her own accord, although I always fell asleep to her awake, staring blankly at the ceiling, and she became vacant and glassy-eyed when I touched or kissed her.

On a warm afternoon, watching a film together, I looked at Serena and felt a flutter in my heart that I hadn't felt for some time. The fact she had stayed alive for some consecutive days was nothing short of a miracle, let alone that she was so calm, too.

"You seem... better," I said, tentatively. I was terrified of throwing off the truce.

"Mm," she responded, non-commital.

"What changed?"

Serena thought for a while. "It wasn't working."

"What do you mean?"

"Well, just that. It wasn't working. If I'm going to come back anyway, why bother trying?"

I bit my lip, but stopped myself from prying further.

I took some days' holiday off work - "It'll be nice to keep you company," I said to Serena - and we spent a day looking for weird shops, finding some matching snail ornaments that we placed on the nightstand proudly. I was still cautious to avoid anyone we knew seeing her, and I made excuses not to go out again, but I felt more at ease and more, well, *normal* than I had for a while.

The day before I was due back at work, I came home to a wonderful smell and Serena buzzing around the kitchen.

"That smells great!" I said, wrapping my arms around her waist. "What is it?"

"It's a stew with a red wine sauce. I wanted something warming tonight," she smiled. "We've got some good bread to eat with it, don't we?"

We sat down to eat, and I poured her a glass of wine, kissing her before sitting down.

"Thank you, this looks amazing!" I lifted my wine to toast her, and began to eat. I felt warm inside: we were worlds away from the horror we'd been living only some days prior. "What is this, beef? I don't know what you seasoned it with, but it's delicious. Haven't had anything like it." I chewed for a bit. "I didn't know we had any meat left. I haven't gone shopping for a while."

She tilted her head sweetly. "Don't be silly. We have loads in the shed."

I stared at her, and her gaze didn't falter. Her lips curled into a faint, uncharacteristic smirk. "You don't mean..." I sputtered, and ran to the sink to throw up.

Serena watched me impassively, and kept eating.

For the first time in a while, I cried when I found her hanging in the closet later that night.

I was in the field again. I felt like I hadn't been here for a while, and I hadn't missed it. The wind was stronger now, and hotter; the humidity made my shirt stick to me unpleasantly.

The dog's fur ruffled in the wind, and it walked up to me slowly.

Ah, you're here again.

I stared at it.

People come here when they need something. I would think I had served you enough.

It watched me for a moment, maybe waiting for an explanation. I didn't have one.

Eventually, I spoke: "Please. Make her happy."

I cannot manipulate the emotions of humans. I have explained this before.

"What will stop her killing herself?"

I couldn't tell you, even if I knew. She is a creature of free will. What she does is up to her. Perhaps, in other circumstances, she wouldn't feel inclined to kill herself.

"Make those circumstances happen. I want you to make those circumstances happen."

The dog looked at me for a little longer than I felt comfortable with. **I cannot manipulate the emotions of humans.**

"That's not manipulating emotions! That's... making circumstances!" I sputtered. "You can make my wife appear in my bed every night, but you can't make the world... right? Right for Serena, I mean? That makes no sense!" My nose tingled, like I was about to cry, but no tears would come. My throat was burnt by the hot air.

You don't understand.

"You're right, I don't!" I tried to step towards the dog. I knew full well that, if I tried to fight it, I would be dead, but I couldn't bring myself to care. I wanted to hurt it like it had hurt me. My legs were heavy, though, and I fell to the floor. "There has to be a way to make things right."

Maybe there is. But my powers can only do so much. You should have learnt that by now.

I glared up at its calm face. It had moved closer, and its snout was inches from my face. Its breath was hotter even than the burning wind blowing through the field.

I don't know how you haven't learnt by now.

"Learnt what, you fucking mutt? Learnt *what*?" I spat on the ground and finally cried.

The dog huffed quietly and waited.

You have come back here for a reason.

"I can't keep doing this."

What do you want, then? I can help you, but only if you tell me what you want.

"I want to be done with all of this." I looked down at

my hands, and they were covered in dried blood. It wasn't mine. "I can't keep doing this," I repeated.

I thought about Serena. I thought about her alive. I imagined her smile, her fluty voice, her soft skin, her silky hair that shone like gold in the sun. I remembered the sound of her viola and her giggles when she saw something she liked in one of her weird shops. I thought about her moving ghost-like through the house, face sunken, eyes hollow. I thought about her face buried into my chest, murmuring about death, and the stench of old flesh that forever lingered in my nostrils.

I'd been torturing her.

"I wish I'd never been born," I whispered.

As you wish.

Acknowledgements

Thanks to Luke for thinking up the basic premise and telling me when I was half-asleep. I didn't seem interested in it because I was half-asleep; it was, in fact, a good concept and very fun to write. He also read bits of it as I was going, which was very helpful!

I wrote this almost exclusively listening to *The Mollusk* by Ween. I don't know why, but it worked for me. Good album.

Thank you to Ann, Nat, Dan, and my mum for reading this in its later stages and making sure it made any sense at all. I really appreciate it!

About the author

Lowarn Gutierrez has loved reading their entire life, and wrote countless stories throughout their childhood.

After a long hiatus from writing anything but academic assignments for school and uni, they decided to give writing fiction another go. This is the first thing they've managed to put together.

Lowarn's lifelong tendency towards the macabre and fascination with dreams (and nightmares) are on proud display here. Ironically, as an artist, they struggle to draw anything that isn't at least a little bit cute.

You can follow them on Twitter, where they post nonsense and, sometimes, their art and other creative pursuits: @foxo_cube